For Lily & Arthur

Many thanks to naturalist Tod Winston of NYC Audubon for sharing
his knowledge of how much life there is in an oak tree —K.M

For J.O. —A.F.

THIS IS A BORZOI BOOK PUBLISHED BY ALFRED A. KNOPF

Text copyright © 2022 by Kate McMullan
Jacket art and interior illustrations copyright © 2022 by Alison Friend
All rights reserved. Published in the United States by Alfred A. Knopf, an imprint of Random House Children's Books,
a division of Penguin Random House LLC, New York.
Knopf, Borzoi Books, and the colophon are registered trademarks of Penguin Random House LLC.

Visit us on the Web! rhcbooks.com
Educators and librarians, for a variety of teaching tools, visit us at RHTeachersLibrarians.com

Library of Congress Cataloging-in-Publication Data
Names: McMullan, Kate, author. | Friend, Alison, illustrator.
Title: This is the tree we planted / Kate McMullan; illustrated by Alison Friend.
Description: First edition. | New York: Alfred A. Knopf Books for Young
Readers, 2022. | Audience: Ages 4–7. | Audience: Grades K–1. | Summary: In rhyming text, a classroom of children
watches the tree they planted, and the birds and animals that make their homes in it.
Identifiers: LCCN 2021010144 (print) | LCCN 2021010145 (ebook) | ISBN 978-0-525-57947-2 (hardcover) |
ISBN 978-0-525-57948-9 (lib. bdg.) | ISBN 978-0-525-57949-6 (ebook)
Subjects: LCSH: Trees—Ecology—Juvenile fiction. | Animals—Habitations—Juvenile fiction. | Stories in rhyme. |
Picture books for children. | CYAC: Stories in rhyme. | Trees—Fiction. | Ecology—Fiction. | Animals—Habitations—
Fiction. | LCGFT: Stories in rhyme. | Picture books.
Classification: LCC PZ8.3.M238 Th 2022 (print) | LCC PZ8.3.M238 (ebook) |
DDC 813.54 [E]—dc23

The illustrations were created using mixed media.
Book design by Sarah Hokanson

MANUFACTURED IN CHINA
February 2022   10 9 8 7 6 5 4 3 2 1   First Edition
Random House Children's Books supports the First Amendment and celebrates the right to read.

This Is
the Tree
We Planted

by
Kate McMullan

illustrated by
Alison Friend

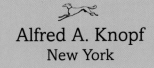

Alfred A. Knopf
New York

This is the TREE

This is the TREE

This is the TREE we planted!

Hey, there's a NEST
that rests in the TREE we planted.

And one, two, three EGGS
inside the NEST
that rests in the TREE we planted.

This must be the ROBIN
that laid the EGGS
inside the NEST
that rests in the TREE we planted.

Look at that SQUIRREL with a thrashing tail

race by the ROBIN

that laid the EGGS

inside the NEST

that rests in the TREE we planted.

Do you hear the KITS? They squeak and wail
calling the SQUIRREL with the thrashing tail
that raced by the ROBIN
that laid the EGGS
inside the NEST
that rests in the TREE we planted.

I see a HAWK with feathers pale

eyeing the KITS that squeak and wail

calling the SQUIRREL with the thrashing tail

that raced by the ROBIN

that laid the EGGS

inside the NEST

that rests in the TREE we planted.

Here come some JAYS zooming over the trail

scaring the HAWK with feathers pale

that eyed the KITS that squeak and wail

calling the SQUIRREL with the thrashing tail

that raced by the ROBIN

that laid the EGGS

inside the NEST

that rests in the TREE we planted.

I spy a SPIDER on silken sail
slide by the JAYS that zoomed over the trail
that scared the HAWK with feathers pale
that eyed the KITS that squeak and wail
calling the SQUIRREL with the thrashing tail

that raced by the ROBIN
that laid the EGGS
inside the NEST
that rests in the TREE
   we planted.

Yikes! That LIZARD with leaf-green scales

ate the SPIDER on silken sail

that slid past the JAYS that zoomed over the trail

that scared the HAWK with feathers pale

that eyed the KITS that squeak and wail

calling the SQUIRREL with the thrashing tail

that raced by the ROBIN

that laid the EGGS

inside the NEST

that rests in the TREE we planted.

Look—

a WALKING STICK as thin as a rail!

a SCARLET TANAGER eating a SNAIL!

a BUTTERFLY with wings so frail!

a WOODPECKER pounding like hammer on nail!

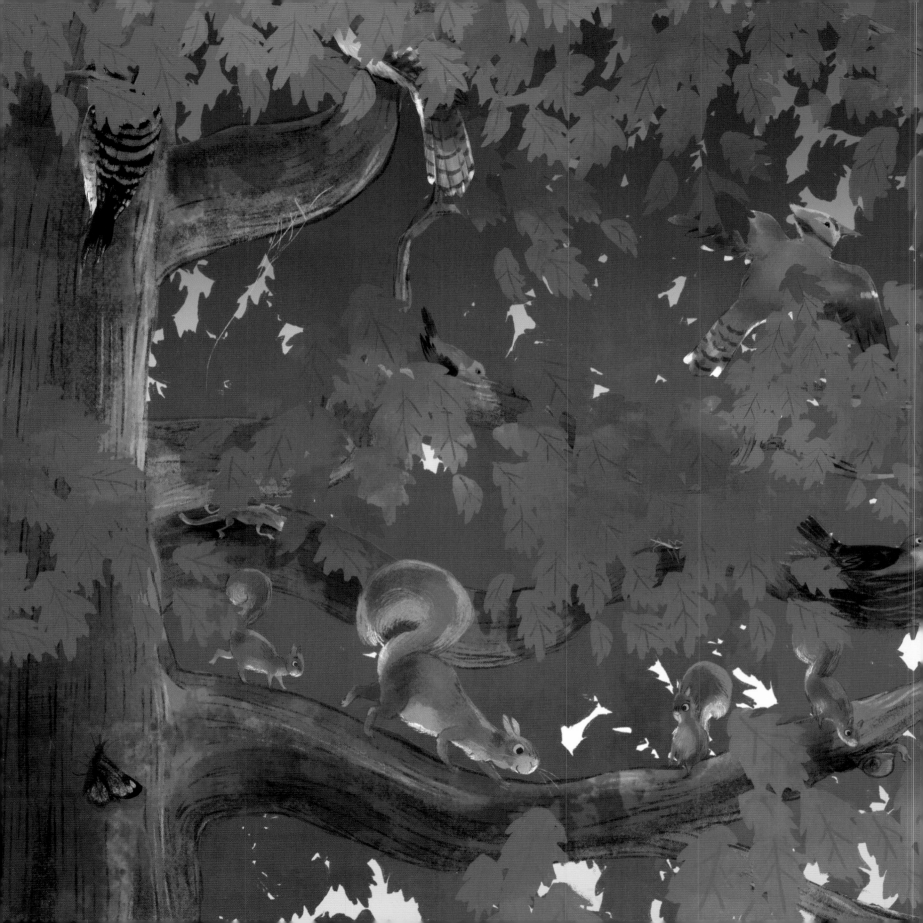

Listen! The OWL from down in the dale

calling *WHOO*

WHOO

WHOO!

WHO planted the tree?

We planted the TREE!

And what did we see?

NEST

EGGS

ROBIN

SQUIRREL

KITS

HAWK

JAYS

SPIDER

LIZARD

WALKING STICK

TANAGER

SNAIL

BUTTERFLY

WOODPECKER

OWL

So many lives are part of the TREE
part of the TREE
All part of the TREE we planted!